Meek

Scene 28

The force of mother nature

Spring a time of renewal

Flames grew from the plug outlets causing the sprinkler system to activate. Steven took off run sprinting towards the stairwell door. "No!" Larry screamed as Steven crossed the shallow flood of water. Leaping up the stairs nearly slipping twice before reaching the top step. Gliding across the water surface to the door of his lab seeing Kevin trying to shut down the system. Getting to the desktop pulling up the bases core network grid shutting down the state's power. The hmm from the powerline faded as the base went dark.

Drops of water fell from every surface the emergency spotlights popped on blinding me. "What's happening?" I asked Maria shielding my eyes. "I don't know," she replied turning her wristlet light on. Fighting the numbing burning sensation coursing through my muscles I sat up. Using gravity to fall into my chair seat using my shaking arms to correct my position. Bands faded into ripples across the water's surface as I made my way to the door. Shedding tears making my way to the office hoping the override allowed Jaz and the kids to escape the air tight room. Bending the corner entering the office Jaz was huddled with the kids under the spotlight in knee high water.

Maneuvering around the desk bracing myself up on the glass window gripping the emergency release leveler. My muscles shook in my arm as I pulled down causing the door to crack open. Water spilled out the opening, Jaz ran to the door yanking it wider. "Come on," Jaz said allowing the kids to pass through first. "What's happening?" Jaz asked squeezing through with AJ in her arms. "I don't know," I replied resting on my elbows. "You need help?" Jaz asked noticing I didn't follow her to the door. "I'm right behind you," I replied forcing myself to sit back. Rolling my eyes gripping my push bars I reversed feeling an electrical current run up my spine.

The water turned bright blue then green, the rolling waves sounded like an approaching tsunami wave. Falling forward landing on my knees covering my ears trying to drown out the pounding rippling waves. "Nay," Josh said covering his ears wobbling around. Jayden took off for the stairs homing in on Nelonnie's racing heartbeat. Arriving at the door Nelonnie was on her knees covering her ears. "Nay," I heard Jayden call out in the distance. Looking around hearing his voice behind me seeing a deep red figure approaching me. Rising from the ground in Jayden's arms he sat me on the desk turning on his wrist light.

"Let me see," he said removing my hand from my ear seeing blue blood all over my fingers. Looking up at him as his light caught my eyes causing a blinding bright flash. "Turn it off!" I yelled shielding my eyes. "Look at me," Jayden said lifting my chin. Opening my eyes his face was outlined with blue rippling light. Everything radiated this rippling blue light the water swaying against the walls lit up the objects hanging. "Maria!" he yelled out turning off his light. Josh was the first through the door stumbling into the chairs and table. "Sit," Thalia said pushing a chair behind Josh. He wasn't bleeding from his ears or eyes like I was yet he kept reaching for his ears.

"Look," Jayden said turning his light on shining it on my face. Josh sucked his teeth flinching as the bright light passed over my eyes. "Nay," Thalia said sounding frighten, concerned, and disgusted. Closing my eyes fighting the shooting pains in my head trying to block out Josh realizing I was hurting him. Every word spoken was like metal banging against metal on my eardrums. Sticking my fingers inside my ears blocking out the noise easing the pounding against my skull. A soft hand rested against my cheek causing me to open my eyes and look up. Maria was standing there looking at me like I was growing a horn out of my forehead. "Her eyes," Cowboy said taking a step back.

"What are your symptoms?" she asked checking my pulse on my wrist. "My ears hurt and everything is blue rippling light," I replied closing my eyes quickly. "Let me see," she whispered pulling my hands away from my head. Slowly removing my hands clinching my teeth as the sound flooded my ear canal. Shining her phone light into my right ear touching the blue blood oozing out. "I need a sample," Ivy said passing maria a cotton ball. Gently dabbing the blood running out of my ear the course texture sounding like nails on a chalkboard. "I need to clean it," she said sounding as if she was yelling through a busted loud speaker.

Soaking a Q-Tip in peroxide softly swabbing around the rim of my inner ear. "Why is it doing that," Ivy asked noticing smoke rising from the Q-Tip and my ear. "Does it burn?" Maria asked watching the blood thicken. Shaking my head no slightly gripping the plexiglass desktop. Using a dry q-tip slowly pushing inside my ear twisting several times then pulling out a long slime tail of clotted blood. "I'm sorry," Maria said seeing blue tears streaming down my face. "Here," Ma'shawn said handing Maria a micro camera. The small light at the end of the microfiber wire vanished as she inserted it in my ear. Looking at the screen as the wire snaked through my canal reaching my eardrum.

"Is it supposed to look like that," Jayden asked as Maria went deeper. Nelonnie screamed pushing Maria's hand away covering her ears. Josh covered his ears falling to his knees blue blood gushing from in between his fingers. "What is it?" Maria asked looking back a Josh on the floor. "It's too loud!" Nelonnie screamed inserting her fingers inside her ears. Steven ran out of the room to his lap grabbing a set of headphones. Returning pushing his way through the on lookers Steven placed the headphones on Nelonnie's head removing her hands then stepped back. All sound faded it was finally quiet my brain stopped pounding against my skull. "What are those?" Jayden asked turning his phone flashlight on.

"You, ok?" Thalia asked Josh as she washed the blood from his hands. "I'm good," he replied standing up wiping his ears. "Let me see that video?" Josh asked curious. Watching the skin heal yet damage Josh didn't understand why he wasn't having the same side effects. Nay pressed on the headphones as her heart beat began to slow. The blue rippling light became steady blue lines everything outlined as if under blacklight. My wrist lit up and vibrated as a message from Steven came through. Looking at the screen then turning away a strong grip froze my arm movement.

Steven adjusted the backlighting on the screen changing the font color a bright neon pink. Better, it said with a smiley face emoji. Everything was clear on the screen even though the wristlet itself was blacked out. Typing causing everyone to fall silent Steven looked up at me then extended his arms complying with my response. Squeezing me tightly his heart racing I squeezed him back thanking him for once again coming to my rescue. "Noise cancelling headphones," Austin said as we released each other. "We need to get the water cleaned up and the power back on," I said loudly causing everyone to look at me crazy.

My wrist vibrated a message from Jayden. You're talking hella loud lol, it read causing me to grin. "Mybad," I said softly waving for my chair. It was awkward watching everyone's lips move but not hear their voices. Receiving constant text messages of the plans in motion. Jayden parked me at the end of a bench table everyone else separated starting their task.

"Your jaw is tight," Jayden said touching my face. "I'm fine," I replied whispering trying to relax my face. "What does it feel like," he asked interlocking our fingers. "At first everything was loud the slightest breeze sounded like a volcano erupting in the middle of a hurricane then everything went dark my brain pounded against my skull I thought I was turning," I replied swallowing the building emotion in my throat.

"Well, you're not bleeding from your ears anymore," he replied turning my head. "You sound like you're talking through a slow leak in an air mattress," I explained pressing the headphones against my ears. His face was outlined perfectly every line and wrinkle visible in blue light. He was smiling looking at me as if he was fascinated causing me to smile. "Why are you staring like that?" I asked causing him to wave his hand in front of my face. Grabbing his wrist stopping him from being a childish stereo type shaking my head. "Don't make me break it," I said easing my grip. "You always get a cool super power," he replied slipping out my grip holding his hand up.

Placing my hand on his creating a greenish orange discharge. "What?" Jayden asked seeing me stare at our hands amazed and confused. "The color it changed," I replied increasing my pressure causing the color to phase greenish yellow. Looking around the lobby as people came and went changing the colors of the solid objects. "Vibrations," I blurted out releasing his hand turning around enjoying the light show. Each vibration gave off a different color the louder the noise the brighter the light. "I can see sound," I announced looking over the rows of canned food. Steven and Kevin came from the stairwell going back and forth about the way to fix the generator.

"You could start an electrical fire setting everything connected to the powerlines we something to ground the current," Kevin said showing Steven his tablet. Steven swiped the screen several times his eyes brows frowning biting his bottom lip as he did when he was thinking. "Tires man you're like the tech lab partner I always wanted," Kevin said grinning at the screen walking up the hall. Looking back at Jayden touching his over grown hair. "Why are you looking at me like that?" I asked as he held his phone up snapping a picture.

"You look like a mine dweller from generation z with those big black eyes," he replied chuckling snapping several more pictures. Covering the light with my hand lowering the phone from my face smirking. "Take another picture and I'll punch you in the face," I said smiling no longer upset at another change only I was going through. Turning his wristlet snapping another picture quickly grabbing my approaching left hand stopping me from hitting him. "You are an ass dude," I said shaking my head smiling uncontrollably at his childish playing. "But you love me though, he replied before kissing me twice. "Something like that," I replied dodging his kiss. "Ugh let's go," Jiayvon said pulling Jayden by the back of his shirt. The younger kids scattered bath towels on the lobby floor sliding on them like mats from the amusement park.

Floral scented bleach phased out the still water smell as Sam and Maria mopped the floors staying ahead of the possible mold growth. The wall outline flickered as the water dried no longer having the motion sounds to be visible to me. Slowly spinning around seeing the kids scooting over the floor at the end of the hall then tossing the navy-blue large cotton towels down the stairs. Looking to my right hearing the squishy sound of the mop head. Behind me probably three feet Hulk was trotting up the hall his nails making a rhythmic pattern with every paw impact. Resting his large head on my lap drooling nudging my hand twice. "I see you boy," I said scratching behind his floppy ears kissing his head.

Sound was all around us the slightest breeze against every surface gave off a different vibration a constant symphony of music. Hulk's tail went stiff the hair rose along is spine but he whined as if he was scared. Turning heading to the large window at the end of the hall a low rumbling in the ground sent ripples through the fields. Reaching the window looking out at the field amazed by the light show. Something was coming from the west it was strong and shaking the ground. After three minutes a large herd of elk ran across the field onto the road running into the mountains. Everyone watched in aww, this was the first time any of us had seen a elk let alone any forest animal.

Hulk began to bark causing everyone to snap out of the moment. As the last few elk made their way onto the paved road a bio leaped onto the young males back causing him to fall over. "Runners!" I yelled as a mass horde of runners tackled the elk at the back of the herd. Those outside ran inside, Jaz took the kids and elderly to the panic room. Watching the bios tear into the five elk I hoped they'd feed and leave. Tayleeyah brought me my weapons harness clutching her small field knife. "Huh no," Maria said taking hold of one of the straps. "You can't see or hear you need to get to the safe room you guys too," Maria snapped tugging on the harness.

"We got this," I replied touching her hand pulling the harness free. The bios began to screech twitching before bursting into flames. "What's happening to them?" Kelli asked leaning on the frame. "I don't know," Sam replied looking confused at the flash burning creatures. "The birds they're still giving off electricity," I announced seeing the charging currents colliding inside the dead birds. "Go get Steven,' I said looking at the birds forming an idea. Tayleeyah and Kelli took off running through the stairwell doors gliding over every other step giggling from the gravity shift in their stomach's. Sliding into the lobby nearly knocking over a pamphlet tower.

Looking back to see what caused the noise the girls straighten their faces speed walking towards Steven. "Nay wants you," they said in unison then racing towards the door giggling. Speeding up the stairs leaping over the rails tagging each other as they climbed to the third floor. Arriving at the door at the same time interlocking their fingers walking in together followed by Steven and Kent. "Those birds are giving off electricity can you use them to jump the generators?" I asked watching the currents building inside the birds. Staring at his screen for several minutes then looked up nodding. "How do we pick up electric birds?" Kent asked looking out at the bios.

Steven walked off no doubt already forming a plan and wasn't waiting to explain. "What if the bio's see us?" Tayleeyah asked causing me to hold my breath. "We can power everything down and only power the grid panel for now," Kent said swiping his tablet screen. "Please do that," I replied wishing I could drown out the chewing sounds. Hulk's heart raced as he restrained himself from barking. Two hours later only bones remained of forest animals slain on the freeway. Steven had created a large tinfoil box to hold the birds in attaching the jumper cables to a rod then the generator. A low discharge noise came from the container of birds as they filled it to the top sealing it finally.

Flipping the switch on the generator a small electrical spark shot from the rods of the generator. The gears began to rotate causing the energy gauge to rise to 15 percent. Steven slammed his fist against the generator. Rolling my eyes removing the cap from my water bottle taking a swig before wasting my ration. "Do it again on my count," I announced rolling towards the box. "On three," I said locking my wheels. "What are you doing?" Jayden asked as Steven gripped the switch tossing the water onto the foil sparks flew as the meter climbed to 34percent. The birds burst into flames Steven quickly flipped the switch off jumping back. Kev sprayed the box with the fire extinguisher.

The gears continued to turn the led panel began to glow red. "Is that a good thing?" I asked waving the smoke from my face coughing. Steven wiped the foam from the panel revealing the power gage. 32percent the meter read blinking at the top cube block. "The panels will charge it up more tomorrow hopefully," Kent said kicking the jumper cables. "Alright let's eat and start over tomorrow," Sam said sticking her head in the room. Filing into the hall realizing with the added group we need to think of a better sleeping arrangement. Counting heads dividing them by rooms on this floor not getting a desired result. My chair stopped then I was spinning around.

Jayden kneeled down locking my breaks biting his bottom lip which meant he was pissed. "Aye don't just play with your life like that," he snapped looking me square in the eyes not blinking. "One, rubber wheels I was fine second I don't play with my life ever and you honestly think I'm going to check in with you every time something drastic needs to happen you don't know me at all," I snapped going for my brake handles. "I'm not saying," Jayden snapped squeezing my hands stopping me. "Look Nay I know your super kick ass but until your eye balls are back to normal can you focus on healing," he replied releasing my hands thumping my nose.

Rolling my eyes but smirking at his serious face I released the brakes rolling backwards nodding my head before turning around. Five of the six picnic tables were now filled spacing was definitely my first priority tomorrow. "So, what's the plan for this?" Jayden asked sliding onto the bench. "Everybody gets an air mattress pick a spot in the hall and we'll figure it out tomorrow," I replied putting my head on the table.

"You know it's time to get stable clean the houses and fence off a neighborhood spread out," he commented kicking my front wheel. "We'll go look in the morning before everybody starts moving around," I said turning and looking at him.

"I'm moving our bed to your office," Jayden whispered resting his chin on his crossed hands. "Really, how about you go get the other beds first," I replied as Josh and Thalia walked up. "Yea this crazy we definitely need to spread out," Thalia said looking over the group. "I know I was thinking we fence off a neighborhood close but spread out defensible," I replied sitting up checking the time. "What about now?" Josh asked yawning for the second time. "Air mattress in the hall," I replied yawning taking my bowl from Jiayvon. "Ugh alright I need volunteers to help bring stuff upstairs," Josh announced leaning on the table exhausted. Seven people hopped up followed by Jayden and Kev.

"I'll get right tomorrow," I whispered through Josh's thoughts of sleeping. Josh shook his head drained physically several of his fractures weren't healed on his ribs. Walking toward the door as I announced the sleeping arrangements the back of my eyeballs tingled. Rubbing my right eye warm thick fluid oozed from my tear duck. Quickly wiping my hand on my sleeve Josh started drilling me with questions saying he was crying blood too. "Shut up!" I snapped backing away from the table speeding to find Maria. Catching her eye I'm the kitchen nodding for her to come out starting towards my office. "What's wrong?" Maria asked turning on her pen light. "My eyes their tingling and I'm leaking blood again," I explained wiping both eyes showing her my hands.

"I need to look at your eyes," she said pulling out her phone. Nodding my head gripping my push bars Maria focused the light on my eyes snapping several pictures then recording. Everything went dark then grey; every blink was a contrast of black then grey. "I'll be back," she said speeding walking out of the room looking at her phone. The tingling began to sting then burn as if my nerve fibers were on fire. Using the bottom of my shirt applying pressure to my eyes clinching my teeth trying not to scream.

Opening my eyes swirling rainbow patterns blinded me my brain beating against my skull burning. Reapplying my blood-soaked shirt to my eyes Maria did a lite jog up the hall back to the office supplies in hand. "Let me see," she said using her teeth to open a pack of gauges. Soaking the pads with saline she gently wiped around my eyes. "Look at me," she instructed lifting my chin. Turning on her pen she ran the dim light over my eyes twice. Taking pictures then video she returned to removing the blood from my face. "The light is grey now," I said closing my eyes trying not to fall out and scream. "How's your hearing?" she said checking my eyes again pressing on the duct.

Nothing came out but her skin had a dull grey tint to It her clothes were different shades of dark grey. "They don't feel like their being blown in by a hurricane," I replied slowly sliding the large muffs from my ears. Maria froze holding her breath even as I allowed the headphones to rest on my neck. Taking a wet gauze wiping inside my left ear struggling with the caked-on blood. "Here let me," Maria said moving slowly opening another package. "I can hear the glue separating on the plastic," I announced hearing the plastic expand on the inflating air mattresses.

Shining her phone light into my canal I could hear her heart rate increase. "What?" I asked curious to what had her fascinated and nervous. "Your ear drum it's healed but it's thicker like leather almost," she replied twisting the gauze into the canal. Sorry," she said sucking her teeth removing the stained gauze. "You always surprise me when you change, evolve, grow, you know what I mean," Maria said starting on my right ear. "I'm just lucky you have medical training," I replied causing her to stop. "I'm far from a doctor honestly I was a week away from quitting as a nurse I wanted to start my own business," she said cleaning up the wrappers.

"Jokes on us I guess," I replied thinking of all the things I wanted to do. Josh and Jayden entered together chewing on granola bars laughing. "Well, let me see," Josh said curious if he would start experiencing symptoms. Looking over at him as he held his phone up to my face using his screen light instead of the flashlight. "Ughh you're still busted," he said pinching my cheek. "Surprisingly you look good in grey blob," I replied blocking his second attempt. "I guess we wait and see," Maria said shrugging her shoulders. "Always got to be the weirdo," Josh said examining my ears. "Yeah, it's getting tight in here," Maria throughout folding her arms

"I know tomorrow we check out the housing area pick a neighborhood start cleaning give everybody some space," I replied as she started for the door. "Stability," she replied before stepping into the hall. "First light, I said cracking my neck feeling the pressure lifting from my joints. "Right," Josh replied leaning on the desk. "So, we push back the run get camp right get organized then move around," Josh said looking down at his boots. "I'll get the bed," Jayden said jogging out the door. "Is your body rejecting the fusion," my brother asked interrupting my thoughts. "No, I don't know what's wrong," I replied looking at my right hand. "Are you pregnant?" he asked standing up his facial expression stunned.

Smacking my teeth punching his stone firm leg calling him every word for stupid. "Stop I'm just asking," Josh stepping out of my impact range. "Byeee," I said rolling to the other side of the desk. "A father has to be concerned," he said causing me to throw my notebook. The frame of the building groaned as swelling went down in the wood. The thud of the blinking blub sounded as if were under my pillow. Closing my eyes allowing my ears to drift with the sounds identifying the different vibrations.

What makes a home

The two-car caravan drove parallel the car barrier to the only cur der sac block on the base. Nine houses in total the soldiers old camp behind the row. Making notes as Jayden pulled into the driveway surprised by my new hi defi grey vision. "So," Josh said opening my door Hulk leaping out. "Bedroom count, addresses, and temporary fencing around the block but it will work," I replied typing quickly. "We'll start on the fences I'll have Ma'shawn get your numbers and we load up everything bring it down here," Josh said looking around at the work. "I want to go check out hq2," I said looking at Thalia.

"I'll take her," she said climbing over me into the driver seat. Jiavyon climbed into the back seat followed by hulk swinging his thick tail. "Ten minutes," Josh snapped closing my door looking at us Suspicious. Peeling off driving onto the grass around the house across the small field around the perimeter gate to the opening. The strong odor of death welcomed us as we made our way into the sitting room. Mounds of military supplies and ammo cluttered the floors accompanied by trash. "Josh asked me was I pregnant," I blurted unsure why he thought that. "Idiot," Thalia said shaking her head. "Are you?" Jiayvon asked causing us to look at her.

"No," I replied looking confused why this was even a thought. "Well, you been glitching every since my disgusting brother touched you we were all thinking it," she replied shrugging her shoulders. "Wow ok hmm definitely not gross everybody was thinking about it," I snapped blushing trying to keep Josh blocked out. "We stay together," Thalia said kicking spam cans. Rocking as we hit the dipping on the uneven field heading back to the caravan.

Knowing everyone was thinking about what Jayden and I had done was consuming my every thought. Opening my door wishing I could speed walk into the building Jayden appeared with my chair. "What's wrong?" he asked turning up his face scooping me up. "Nothing," I replied smiling kissing his cheek twice. "Hopefully by sundown we have three houses clean," he said playing with Hulk as I adjusted my hips. "Before sundown if we use the pressure washers and the pickups the move the trash," I replied unlocking the brakes. "Big guns, short cuts, dangerous, super bad," Jayden said holding the door open.

Cowboy had the chicken coop in the lobby feeding the roosters and hens. Hulk ran to the gate whining and licking at the animals causing the pen to slide. "Hulk!" I yelled causing an echo but he froze then turned to face me. "Come on leave them alone," I instructed heading for rows of supplies. "Can we share a room?" Kelli asked grabbing items from the shelves. "Sure can in fact you guys can clean your room," I replied filling a trash back with odds and ends. "Trucks nearly full your brother and a few others are already on their way back," Sam said carrying a sealed deep rock bottle.

"Definitely need four or five of those and the large steel tubs," I replied pulling the strings on the overflowing bag. "We need to get them set up soon on dirt and grass," Cowboy announced adjusting the pen placement. "There's a small open field you can build there when you have time," I replied as everyone filed by. "I got the gate," Serg said putting his duffle bag on his lap. "Got my walkie," I said looking around hating the power was out. Sliding into the driver seat of the purple minivan breaking the chair down sliding them over to Tayleeyah. Making my way up the road shaking my head at the roll of cars pulled to the front lot two truckloads were passing by. Small piles of furniture were growing outside the houses.

"Which one is ours?" Tayleeyah asked sitting up looking around excited. "Hold on it's going to get bumpy," I said pulling onto the side walk. Giggling as we dipped then got air the girls gripped each other's hands. Rolling up the driveway stopping in front of the double doors turning the engine off. "Ok we glove up you guys pick a room and get everything outside right there," I instructed opening my door. "It stinks," Kelli said plugging her nose. "I know, I smirked slide out the van looking at all the windows. Opening every window on the first floor the spring breeze blew the curtains.

Sweeping everything into a pile near the door I couldn't believe how gross men were. Juice ran from the meat cans onto my gloves as I stuffed six bags in total. "Can we keep the dressers?" Tayleeyah asked dragging a bag up the hall. "Bleach it down inside and out," I replied making my way to the kitchen. My skin crawled seeing maggots squirm from the bottom of the refrigerator. Starting on the lower cabinets tossing everything swiping the counter tops contains into bags. Sweeping the floor happy hardwood ran through the entire house. Going through five 200 count yard trash bags the curtains, rugs, couch pillows, dining chairs were outside.

Carrying what they could as a team to the pile I dragged and pushed the ugly flower print high back chairs to the door. "This everything going?" Josh asked grabbing the coffee tables tossing them. "The fridge too and whatever's upstairs," I replied looking at the bare floors. "It's hot as fuck yo," Jayden snapped walking through the doorway dripping sweat. "I know once I disinfect, I'll set up the solar fans get some blinds up," I said wiping my neck. "Alright six more trips," Josh said finishing his water tossing the bottle on the grass. Carrying the Victorian style couches out first I now could spray the front of the house.

It was just going on noon and my eyes stung from the hot
bleach water dripping from the molding

Making a list of everything the house needed as the girls
spread towels out on the floor. "I'm hungry," Kelli said through
her face mask. "Go get the bag from the front seat!" I yelled out
as they returned for the last pile of trash. "We'll start on the
fence after we eat," Josh said limping from the driver seat
leaving the door open. "I brought snacks," I announced turning
to face the cars extending my hand for the bag. Untying the
strings everyone's face was in the bag reaching for goodies.
Unfolding Hulks portable bowl filling it as the others fell silent.
Looking over at the neighborhood impressed by the height piles
on the curb.

"Thankful a lot of these people just left not a lot of
structure damage," Josh said inhaling his last bag of chips.
"Once the cleaning is done everybody can shop start decorating
while I work on the store," I replied marking the location. "The
store over the tunnel?" Jayden asked smacking on gummy
bears. "It's enough space for us to eat it has storage space and
access back to the main building," I replied loving the space idea
more. "Shit the fence!" Josh said tossing his chip bag running for
the kitchen. The two carried the stainless-steel double door
refrigerator out to the pickup truck. "Dude this is what was
reeking," Josh said coughing and gagging. "We're behind you!" I
yelled out looking up at the fluffy light grey clouds.

Making our way back onto the road pulling up to Sam
whom was filling up a pressure washer pack. "Three more
houses and we're done," she said emptying a bleach container.
"I'm going to start lunch I'm on the walkie," I informed her
releasing the brake slowly. "Call when it's done," she yelled out
shouldering the pack. Speeding up the side street causing a
cooling breeze the girls stuck their hands out the window.
Arriving to the front lot Cowboy was checking the low hanging

snow plow he somehow attached to a Jeep. "Will it work?" I asked getting into my chair giggling.

"I'm about to find out," he replied climbing into the jeep shifting into reverse. The plow slid across the concrete causing a loud grinding noise until he reached the grass. Reversing down to the car barrier hopping out clearing his path Cowboy reversed untiled he reached the housing car barrier. Entering the lobby cowboy had use plastic to block the animal's view. "Alright we have a lot of stuff we need for the house," I said approaching the row of metal shelves. Running down the list as the girls darted around filling large tubs. "Drag them to the doors," I instructed grabbing cans of chunky stew.

"We're at 56 percent," Kent announced as he and Steven came from the stairwell. "Good we got the houses disinfected I'm about to start lunch," I replied packing a camping stove kit. Opening a single stove cooker propping up a small metal folding table attaching the propane tank igniting a flame ring. Peeling the tops from four large cans dumping them in the warming pan causing a steam cloud. Stuffing the trash inside a bag looking up seeing Cowboy carve out a nice square next to my house. "You need help?" Jay asked appearing next to me followed by a small group. "Yea can you put those tubs in the van," I asked stirring the boiling stew.

Jaz came down followed by the younger kids softly singing row, row, row your boat. "You guys' stink like old onions and dirty socks," Jaz said turning her nose up. "You should start getting housing stuff together so I can take it when I drop this load," I said thinking of her face when she sees the rooms Austin picked. "I made some rice you can stretch stew," she said rubbing her sleeping son's head. "Good just fill up whatever you can and it will get loaded," I replied turning down the heat. The over flowing shelves were growing bare as groups traveled back and forth getting items to set up their space. My focus was our new dining center and getting inside once lunch was over.

Jessica and Barbie pushed wheel barrows filled with gardening tools. "Gonna have cowboy clear the center field in the back start putting up the green houses," Jessica said in motion to the doors. Everybody assigned themselves task and completed them on their own time. The girls took colorful bed sets and matching rugs. "Don't forget window film and lamps!" I yelled out hoping everyone heard me. Giving Hulk a bowl disconnecting the propane tank Josh walked in two shades darker. Grabbing a bowl sipping the stew chewing fast sucking in air.

"I want to check out the store start cleaning up so we can stock everybody up tomorrow," I said taking my last bite rice tew mixer. "We need that furniture," Josh replied leaning on an empty shelf. "As long as the fence is up, we should be good finishing the move," I said thinking getting a few people back on watch. "When we get back, we'll finish the brick walls," Josh said thinking of the billion things he had to do. "Why haven't any bios passed by in a while?" I asked causing his mumbling to stop. A loud bang came from outside causing Josh to stand correctly a group crowding around the barrier.

Making our way outside a thick black cloud rose into the air. Ten or twenty miles away from the base balls of fire shot into the air followed by several explosions. "D'sean go get Steven and a drone," I instructed looking over the map on my wristlet trying to guesstimate the location. "Alright we got stuff to do we're losing daylight," Sam said causing everyone to turn away. "Wat, you think it is," Jayden asked shielding his eyes from the sun.

Steven and Kent went out gently placing the large flying toy on the ground. Walking towards me focused on the screen

Steven tapped the joystick causing the blades to spin. Clearing the fence speeding across the field gaining altitude heading for the site. Bio's maze through the streets making their way to the source of the loud explosion. Fighting the strong wind currents pasting over apartments and house's ending up over a large fenced in field. "The Airport," Josh said as a crowd of flaming bios wondered around the fuel tanks. "Can you get close to a window so we can see inside?" I asked wishing he would lower the screen. Heading for the fourth story window Christmas lights blinked hanging around the food courtyard. "Survivor's," Thalia said as dark figures ran behind the seats facing the window.

A young girl no older then 10 slowly approached the window staring at the drone. "Zoom in," I instructed wanting to see more of their set up. The young girl slammed her hand on the window causing all of us to flinch. She pointed down so steven changed the direction of the camera. Running bios were climbing on top of each other creating a tower to the drone. Backing away from the window as a bio swiped the camera the drone wobbled hen steadied. "Come back," I instructed surprised the Airport was still intact. "We should go," Josh said anxious to get back out there.

"We'll talk at dinner," Thalia said biting her bottom lip. Heading back to the house dropping off load after load of supplies I watched the time fly bye. The solar spot lights lit up each floor of every house in the cult da sac. Solar string garden lights gave a soft dim to the 9ft tall post at each corner of the plowed field. Cowboy placed the three coop houses on the corner area of the dugout field extending the metal link fence giving them more room to roam. It was 8pm the sun was disappearing behind the peaks.

"Two more hours," I announced over the walkie talkie knowing we all had to vote on the airport move. Tossing boxes from the pot and pan sets aligning them under the cabinets. Making the twin sizes beds divided by a four-drawer dresser top with spinning unicorn and star lamps. Turning on the hanging butterfly lights strung around the room the girls high fived as the colorful lights illuminated their room. Jaz stuffed teddy bears at the head of AJ's crib smiling as Austin drilled the last nail into the nursery door, the only entry to the carriage bathroom and nursey.

"It almost feels real," Jaz said rubbing her stomach turning on the hanging string baseball lights. "It is real," he said wrapping his arms around her swollen belly. "Our love is real we found each other you're the mother of our beautiful children we are a part of a strong family despite everything we're together keep fighting for that," he whispered kissing the forehead of his nursing son rubbing and kissing her belly. "My feet hurt," she said rubbing his face then kissing him softly. "Let's get you guys to the truck," he said turning the lights out interlocking their fingers. "Wow Nay, it look's great we need furniture now," Jaz said seeing the new curtains.

"Tomorrow we should be comfortable," I replied thinking of the young girl. "What's in here?" she asked opening the double doors to the nook area off the dining room. "An extra room," I replied shining my phone light on the bags of supplies. The girls ran to the van talking about the tv they wanted starving and tired. The caravan maze, its way back to the front building excited about the move. The hall was crowded everyone grabbing plates searching for a seat as I set the computer. More people could draw bio's the risk grew higher with stubborn people. "Alright," I said loud enough for everyone to fall silent.

"The grid will be operational tomorrow but we still have to prioritize," I said pulling up the drone footage. "On a serious note, the explosions were from fuel tanks at the airport," I announced playing the video. All sound faded as everyone watched the young girl bang on the window. The video looped several times no one chewing on the veggie spaghetti. "So, you know we decide everything as a family the floor is open," I announce mixing my sauce.

"What now?" D'sean asked tossing his empty paper bowl. "Every voice count's," I replied tapping the space bar. It was decided Josh and the older group would go for the airport and D'sean and the younger teens would ride with Deborah at first light. Deflating the beds piling into the waiting cars half of the group turned to the housing area. Jayden had the sheets pulled tight the pillow's fluffed and small led tea lights on the desk. Peeling out of my clothes Jayden gripped my tank top stopping me from pulling it over my head. His lips pressed against mine finishing the removal process.

It was like saying good bye and hello at the same time as my nails slid on his sweaty skin. Pure bliss couldn't change the reality he was leaving for a long time. Laying on his chest listening to his racing heartbeat slow down wishing time would freeze. "So, I heard Josh thought you were pregnant," he said moving the hair from my face. Giggling looking up at his smiling face turning my lips up nodding my head. "He said I've been glitchy every since so he was just checking," I explained amused. "Oh, the whole group thought so too," I added causing him to shake his head but smirking.

"Naw we're not ready for all of that," Jayden said placing his feet on mine. "Right why is it a topic it's weird," I replied wiggling my toes. "You think that might be the reason your eyes changed?" he asked sitting up all expression leaving his face. Pulling myself up trying so hard not to laugh seeing he really thought he did something wrong. "Dude alien DNA and all losing my virginity wouldn't change me I think it was to understand the flaw in my genetics and tried fix it but it can't," I replied rubbing my neck. "You still get memories?" he asked causing all my thoughts to freeze. "The Klan leader so was promised to he's going to weak in any vessel that he bonds with because he spread his self-thin creating the bio's he thought my dna could alter his what if he's right," I replied concerned about what she's been showing me.

"Until he shows his self we focus on the mission but as soon as he does I'm taking his head and burning the body myself," Jayden said his jaw muscle tightening. Laying my head on his shoulder as he wrapped his arm around my neck pulling me closer. "Two," he blurted out tapping on my fingers like a piano. "Two what?" I asked checking the time on his wrist. "Kids a boy and a girl," Jayden said causing me to sit on the edge of the bed. "What?" he asked grabbing my hand. "I can barely protect myself how could I take care of one baby let alone two I shouldn't put them in danger I shouldn't have kids," I replied sliding his shirt on.

"Nope come here," he said pulling me back into the bed. "Nay you've nearly died for kids that aren't your family, you stay ten steps ahead of everyone with your stubborn hard headed ass, your passion and that savage brain you're going to be the best mom ever," he said hugging me. "Stop thinking so much just fight, fight for bringing all those ideas in that big ass head to life so everybody sees the future you see," he said releasing his hold kissing and licking my cheek. "Your wack," I said dodging his last kiss. Low voice tones came from the hall as Kev started several coffee pots. "I guess it's time to get ready," Jayden said sneaking a kiss.

Jayden joked the entire time we dressed keeping me from getting emotional. "Maybe we can have a whole chicken spread when you guys get back," I interrupted causing his stomach to growl loudly. "Definitely need a thanksgiving style deal with hella biscuits," he replied pulling the bottom half of the suit over his hips. Folding the blankets as he deflated the high rise air bed the voice tone level rose as everyone was up and packing. Joining the others Maria and Sam were bringing up boxes of variety pack instant oatmeal and powder milk.

 "We eat then head out," Cowboy announced heading down to check on the chickens. "Alright who's going where?" Ivy asked blowing on her coffee. "Josh's group is going to the airport D'sean's group is taking over supply runs," I said opening my notebook. "Run it down professor X," Tay'sean yelled out getting a few laughs. Going over the days agenda as the sun rose behind the purple clouds. Going over the list five times with the new runners Josh gave laws once outside the fence a only one rule everybody comes back. "When do we get xmen suits?" Alex asked waving his hand

 Ma'shawn slapped him in the back of the head as the large pots of steaming oatmeal arrived. The group was adapting well volunteering for work enjoying the distractions, I guess. Josh was anxious to get back to the fight given in to the primal instincts of both human and alien. The base was a mess honestly, I'm surprised we haven't been raided or over ran yet. I can see in black and white and then power should be on by noon. "Alright I'm about to move the animals I could use your help and truck," Cowboy pointing at Carlos. "Let's get it done," Carlos replied scooping the last of his oatmeal up. "That's our que," Deborah said handing me Brazil.

 "I'm taking a to go bowl," Tay'sean said filling his bowl to the rim. "Us too," the teens said crowding around the table scrapping the pots. "Be careful out there I'm trusting you guys for some dumb reason," I yelled out as they ran for the door. "So now what?" Jaz asked looking around at the rest of us. "Well now that they're out the way, Jess needs help getting all gardening stuff from the shelves and second building to the greenhouse," Stacy AND Melisa rose their hands. "Right on find cars that start load them, I need the neighborhood mini market sanitized top priority," I said looking at the remaining group. "We can do that," the man with salt and pepper hair said his family standing up.

"There's cleaning products in the minivan find a car head for the store, and restocking and bricking the fence is left," I announced to the remaining five. "What do I have to do for the fence?" the woman asked holding on to her teenage son's hand. "Laying cement expanding the wall," I replied as the three elderly people pushed their bowls away. "Not you three you guys help with the kids and organizing," I said smiling easing their facial expressions. "If you want to go with the kids your age you can I'll be alright," the mom said hesitating releasing his hand.

"You'll be inside the fence surrounded by all of us and he's with a smart group," I said seeing his grip go limp. Taking giant steps forward he didn't look back knowing she was making a face. Finally, their hands disconnected he sped walk towards the door. "Second floor," I yelled out collecting dishes. She clinched her fist frozen turning pale. "Can you get that pot?" I asked causing her to exhale finally. "Me?" she asked focused on the closing door. "Yea there's storage containers in the for whatever's left," I announced to the man with salt and pepper hair quickly clearing his table.

His wife smiled as he sped table to table shelf to shelf humming softly. Taking the stack of bowls from the tables woman headed for the kitchen humming the same tune as her husband. You would have more space if you turned your smaller cans, the pale woman said turning the peas. "Nelonnie but Nay is fine," I said extending my hand. "Tiffani with an I," she said shaking my hand. "We'll we have mountains of stuff and I really need help setting everything up so we can grab and go," I explained rolling pass the wall of confusion. "Do you have black tape?" Tiffani asked removing everything from a top shelf on to the table.

Removing the rails placing them wider apart the laying the boards down. "Duck or gorilla is all we got," I replied pointing to the stack on the brochure stand. "Can I move these stands too?" she asked counting the tiles on the floor. "You got this we'll get out your way," I said backing up. "Mrs. what's your name," I asked as she carried a large bucket of water out placing it center floor. "Winnie, my grand babies called me Winnie and he's my better have poppa j," she replied dipping the mops. Poppa j began sweeping up and down the hall in uniform pattern moving the stands and displays to one side.

Dancing with the dust mop compiling a pile larger than I excepted sweeping the hall myself twice. "I was a janitor for 47 years I've cleaned everything from slaughter houses to the office of the people until they forced me to retire," he said adding the linen fresh scent disinfected to the steaming water. "Can you start over here I'll move the shelves?" Tiffani asked sliding the smaller towers right. "Sure, can let me help you," Poppa j said moving the towers with ease. Heading for my office Jaz opened the second door allowing the younger kids to play. "Is there any more of that type of stuff in storage?"

"Ton's," I replied thinking of her face when she seen the baby stuff. "Can you?" she said extending AJ. "Of course," I replied taking him smiling. Everyone was off prepping to head out, the base would be half capacity once both groups left. Steven stood in the doorway wearing a suit gripping a helmet a plastic pack strapped to his shoulders. "Generator," I asked still stunned every time he gears up. Typing on his wristlet walking toward me he looked at the desk tapping on the black screen. "89 percent by noon everything should be operational," he replied finally looking at me. "Does Kent know how to fix everything and get into your programs?" I asked adjusting AJ.

Focused on the screen his facial expression never changed it never has. Looking up tapping his leg the computer read out. "He's good I like him," he said shocking me. Steven with an actual emotion and even maybe calling someone friend. "Soon as we're operational I'll patch you in be careful out there look out for them," I said hearing deb's rig start. Reaching over hugging us tightly then running off. "Ok," I said feeling like I'm in the multiverse. "Are you guys doing this?" I asked AJ and the other kids wishing I could see the colorfully flashing lights on the toys.

The mixture of scents poppa j created overpowered every odor the building ever held. Dancing pass the door moving his bucket as he mopped in sections. Metal creaking as the fence opened the jeeps pulling out first. 9am, marking their time they all left reminding myself every five hours to check the time. The light from the rising sun reflected perfectly brightening the hall as if the lights came on. "She totally downplayed the storage floor," Tiffani said dropping several bags on the table. Turning to retrieve more items from the medium size mound she left Winnie winked at her husband and followed Tiffani out.

Climbing over the edge of the mount of bags and boxes Winnie entered second. All praise to the universe, Winnie said grabbing pots sets she dreamed of buying. Spice racks, knife sets, large containers, her dream kitchen was in reach causing her to shed tears. "Start a pile behind mine I'll help you," Tiffani yelled giggling starting stacking what she could creating paths. "Much better," Jaz said entering the room with a tall plastic clothes hamper. "I'm searching for the metal shelves now," Tiffani replied creating random towers. "There's an isle behind those bags to your right," Jaz explained making her way through the maze.

Two bags went flying in the air along with Tiffani's legs followed by the mound of trash bags. "Hold on we're coming," Winnie giggled climbing over piles moving bags. The women laughed falling over but digging her out. "You ok sweety I apologize for laughing," Winnie asked seeing Tiffani's face finally. Tiffani was laughing so hard tears ran from her eyes taking the extended hands pulling herself up. Looking around at the mess the trio laughed hard.

"I never thought clutter could make me so happy right now," Tiffani said wiping her face smiling for the first time since the outbreak. "These are teenagers of course this place is a mess," she said fanning her arms on the mess. The teens were taking their rite of passage retrieving supplies for the base. Josh was headed for D.I.A airport a major strong hold if the inhabits are willing to merge. The base is under staffed over supplied and vulnerable but once the power returned a slim advantage is possible. Operation restart was in full effect and regardless of what happened before the base, finding each other, fighting for each other and a better tomorrow for those that adapting was inside of us along, human, alien didn't matter right now.